Dirty Bertie

BEES!

For Poots McToots ~ D R
For Harry Fitzgerald ~ A M

STRIPES PUBLISHING LIMITED
An imprint of the Little Tiger Group
1 Coda Studios, 189 Munster Road,
London SW6 6AW

Imported into the EEA by Penguin Random House Ireland,
Morrison Chambers, 32 Nassau Street, Dublin D02 YH68

A paperback original
First published in Great Britain in 2021

Characters created by David Roberts
Text copyright © Alan MacDonald, 2021
Illustrations copyright © David Roberts, 2021

ISBN: 978-1-78895-113-5

Printed a...

The For... ...cated
to the p... ...rds
based o...
environ...

10 9 8 7...

Dirty Bertie

BEES!

DAVID ROBERTS WRITTEN BY ALAN MACDONALD

LITTLE TIGER
LONDON

Dirty Bertie
Collect all the
Dirty Bertie books!

Contents

BEES!

CHAPTER 1

Bertie was having breakfast with his family. He spread a thick splodge of honey on his toast and bit into it.

"Mmm, nishe honey," he said, licking his lips.

"Actually, that's Mr Monk's honey," said Dad.

"Mr Monk makes honey?" said Bertie.

"Yes, at least his bees do," replied
Dad.

Bertie was amazed. He had no idea
that Mr Monk, the grouchiest neighbour
on their street, kept bees.

"Where does he keep them, in his
bedroom?" asked Bertie.

Suzy rolled her eyes.

"He's got a beehive in the garden,"
explained Dad.

Bertie's eyes lit up. A beehive! Why
had no one ever told him you could
keep bees as pets? He'd had all kinds of
pets, including worms, fleas, mice and
a spider, not to mention Whiffer – but
bees would be even better! For a start
they'd be the easiest pets in the world.
You didn't have to take bees for a walk
or clear up their poo from the garden!

Dirty Bertie

Bees would just buzz around happily all day making you loads of yummy honey.

"How do you get the honey?" he asked. "Do the bees make it in jars?"

Suzy put her head in her hands.

"No, the bees collect pollen and make honeycomb in their hive," explained Mum, wiping the table. "It takes a lot of time and patience to produce honey."

Bertie didn't think it could be that complicated – bees made honey and he was happy to eat it – what could be simpler?

"So could we get some bees?"

"Definitely not," said Dad.

"Don't even think about it," said Mum.

"Why not?" asked Bertie. "I don't mind looking after them."

"Bees aren't pets," said Mum. "You have to know what you're doing or you'll get stung. Ask Mr Monk, he'll tell you."

Bertie thought he might just do that. His parents would come round to the

Dirty Bertie

idea once they started getting free
honey. Perhaps Mr Monk could help him
get started with a few bees of his own?
There was just one problem: Mr Monk
didn't like Bertie. There had been one
or two little accidents in the past, such
as the time Bertie destroyed Mr Monk's
model dinosaur. But surely he would
have forgotten by now…

CHAPTER 2

All through school Bertie kept thinking about getting some bees. It was amazing that they could make honey. In time maybe he could teach them to make jam and peanut butter too? On the way home he explained his plan to Darren and Eugene.

"Bees?" said Darren. "What do you

want bees for?"

"They'd make great pets," explained Bertie.

Eugene pulled a face. "I don't like bees, I got stung by a wasp once. It crawled inside my sock."

"Bees aren't as stingy," Bertie argued. "If you give them their own beehive they're happy just to make honey for you."

"Honey *is* yummy," admitted Darren.

"Exactly, and it's dead easy to make," said Bertie. "You just say to the bees 'More honey please, bees', and they get to work."

Eugene frowned. "It can't be that easy."

"It is if you've got bees," claimed Bertie. "Anyway, why don't we ask Mr Monk? He's got millions – I'm sure he can spare a few."

"Mr Monk? No way!" said Darren. "Not after last time."

"He chased us out of the park," said Eugene. "Don't you remember?"

Bertie did remember. Mr Monk was head gardener in the park and they'd dug up his rose beds looking for gold. Still, anyone could make a mistake.

"It'll be fine," said Bertie. "Come on."

Twenty minutes later they reached Mr Monk's house and stopped outside.

"Do we have to?" sighed Eugene. "He'll probably start yelling at us again."

Dirty Bertie

"We're only asking to see his bees,"
said Bertie. "If I make my own honey,
you can have the first jar."

He reached up and rang the doorbell.

"He's out. Let's go," said Eugene,
turning away.

But just then the door swung open.
Mr Monk was wearing his work overalls.
He didn't look pleased to see them.

"Oh, it's you," he grunted. "What do you want?"

"Hi, Mr Monk," said Bertie. "My dad says you've got bees."

"What if I have? That's my business," snapped Mr Monk.

"We were just wondering if we could see them?" asked Bertie.

"No you can't," replied Mr Monk, starting to close the door.

Bertie shot out his hand to stop it shutting in their face.

"We won't touch anything," he promised.

"We're just interested," said Darren.

"Why?" demanded Mr Monk. "What are you after?"

"Nothing!" said Bertie. He put on his most earnest expression, the one he used on teachers when he was in trouble.

"I love bees," he said. "I've always wanted to see a real beehive and learn how they make honey. We've been doing it at school, haven't we?"

"Have we?" asked Eugene. Bertie elbowed him in the ribs.

Mr Monk folded his arms. Generally he didn't like children, especially grubby little pests like Bertie. Still, he was very proud of his bees and he was flattered that someone was taking an interest. Maybe he could teach them a thing or two?

"Well all right, I guess there's no harm in letting you see them," he said. "But on one condition – you do *not* touch anything, is that clear?"

CHAPTER 3

Mr Monk led them down the garden. The beehive was tucked behind the shed at the bottom. It looked like a tiny wooden house sitting on a platform.

"Wow!" cried Bertie. "Are all the bees in there?"

"Don't touch it!" warned Mr Monk. "Never go near a beehive unless you know what you're doing."

Eugene and Darren hung back but Bertie was keen to see the bees making all that yummy honey. He could hear a faint buzzing coming from the hive.

"Bees are clever creatures, they all work together," said Mr Monk. He began explaining in great detail about queen bees, worker bees and drones. Darren yawned while Eugene nodded politely. Bertie soon lost interest and turned his attention to a white suit hanging on the shed door with a large hat and gloves.

"And that's why I always wear my beekeeper's outfit," Mr Monk finished. "Of course I use a smoker too, so the bees stay calm. I'll show you."

He disappeared into the shed to fetch it.

While Mr Monk was busy Bertie took
the chance to try on his beekeeper's
hat. It had a net that pulled down to
cover your face.

"Is this what you wear?" he asked as
Mr Monk reappeared.

"Put that back!" barked Mr Monk, grabbing his hat. "I thought I told you not to touch anything."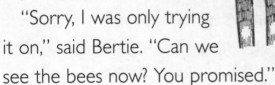

"Sorry, I was only trying it on," said Bertie. "Can we see the bees now? You promised."

Mr Monk sighed. Children these days had no patience. He pulled on his beekeeper's suit, hat and gloves. Bertie watched as he puffed smoke into the hive with the smoker.

At long last Mr Monk was ready.

"Right, stand well back," he warned.

Carefully he opened the roof of the beehive. The buzzing grew louder.

BUZZ! BUZZ! BUZZ!

Dirty Bertie

"Wow! There must be millions!" gasped Bertie.

"Probably close to thirty thousand," said Mr Monk proudly.

"But where's all the honey?" asked Darren. "I can't see it."

"It collects in these frames," explained Mr Monk. He drew one out. It was crawling with bees and covered in a sticky brown gunge.

"First I scrape off the layer of beeswax from the honeycomb, then I scoop out the honey. So there you have it, that's what a beehive looks like," said Mr Monk, returning the frame and closing the roof.

Eugene came out from behind the shed where he'd been hiding.

"Amazing!" said Bertie. "Actually I'm thinking of getting some bees myself."

Mr Monk stared. "YOU?"

"Yes, just a few to get started," said Bertie.

"You don't know the first thing about it," said Mr Monk.

"I could learn," argued Bertie. "I just need some bees of my own. You've got thousands."

"Oh no," said Mr Monk. "I wouldn't trust you with a caterpillar let alone any of my bees. Now the show's over, time to go home."

"Well that's that then," said Darren, when they found themselves back outside Mr Monk's house. "No bees and no honey."

"I told you he wouldn't help," said Eugene. "He's such an old grump-bag."

"Maybe we could catch some bees of our own?" suggested Bertie.

"Huh! Good luck with that!" scoffed Darren.

"I'm not getting stung," said Eugene.

Bertie sighed. He'd been looking forward to keeping bees and eating his own honey. He'd even thought of the perfect place for them: Suzy's old doll's house, which was collecting dust in a cupboard. The bees could have their own bedrooms and buzz up and down stairs. There had to be some way to get his hands on some!

Back at Bertie's house, they trooped into the kitchen.

"Ah, perfect timing," said Mum. "I've got a job for you three."

Dirty Bertie

Bertie hoped it wasn't tidying his bedroom – that would take them years.

Mum pointed to a box of jam jars. "I've been collecting these for Mr Monk," she said. "Can you take them round? He promised he'd swap them for a jar of honey."

"Really?" said Bertie. Here was the perfect excuse to go back! And if Mr Monk needed jam jars, maybe he'd throw in a few bees in exchange, as well as the honey?

CHAPTER 4

Ten minutes later they were back at Mr Monk's front door. This time there was no reply at all.

"He's gone out. Pity," said Eugene.

But Bertie headed to the side gate and pushed it open.

"He's probably still in the back garden," he said. "Come on."

Dirty Bertie

They found Mr Monk busy with his beehive. He was bent over with his back to them, wearing his beekeeper's outfit.

"Hi, Mr Monk!" cried Bertie loudly.

Mr Monk swung round startled, clutching the smoker in his hand.

"Not you again!" he groaned.

"My mum asked us to bring you these jam jars," said Bertie.

"Oh, I see," said Mr Monk. "Just leave them by the shed."

He waited for them to go.

"She said you'd swap them for a jar of honey," Bertie reminded him. He decided to wait till he'd got the honey before mentioning the bees. Maybe Mr Monk would return in a better mood?

Mr Monk sighed and put down the smoker. "Wait there and don't touch

anything," he said, taking off his hat
and gloves before disappearing into the
house.

Bertie stared at the hive. The bees
buzzed noisily, almost as if they were
calling to him. *What if a few bees
happened to crawl into a jam jar?* he
thought. That wouldn't be his fault.
Besides, when you thought about it,
bees didn't really belong to anyone, so
it wasn't like he was stealing them.

He picked up the hat and gloves and
put them on.

"What are you doing?" hissed Darren.

"He told us not to touch anything!"
said Eugene.

"Shh! I'm only going to take a look,"
said Bertie. "Keep an eye out for him
coming back."

He crept closer to the beehive and slowly raised the roof. The buzzing grew louder.

BUZZ! BUZZ! BUZZ!

"You're crazy! You'll get us all stung!" squawked Darren, retreating to the shed. Eugene hid behind him.

"You're meant to use the smoker," he said. "Otherwise the bees get angry!"

"Relax!" said Bertie, who hadn't listened to a word of Mr Monk's lecture. He decided the best way to keep the bees calm was to sing a lullaby.

Dirty Bertie

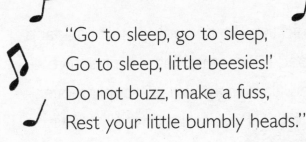

"Go to sleep, go to sleep,
Go to sleep, little beesies!'
Do not buzz, make a fuss,
Rest your little bumbly heads."

The bees however didn't seem sleepy
and buzzed even louder. Bertie picked
up a jam jar and tried to coax one
or two to crawl inside. It wasn't easy.
Suddenly he heard the back door close.
Help! Mr Monk was coming back!

A moment later he appeared
clutching a jar of honey.

"What the…? Get away from there!"
he yelled, staring in horror.

The roof of the hive was still up and
bees were escaping.

"Give me that!" shouted Mr Monk,
trying to grab his hat.

Dirty Bertie

Panicking, Bertie took a step back and bumped into something. The beehive rocked alarmingly, almost toppling over. That did it. Bees started to fill the air – first twenty, then fifty, till they were pouring out in their thousands.

"Yikes!" said Bertie. He threw the hat at Mr Monk and ran to join his friends.

Mr Monk jammed it on his head and tried desperately to close the roof.

"NO! NOOOO! STOP!" he wailed.

It was too late. The bees were now a swarm, streaming out and rising into the sky. They formed a dark cloud high above them and then came sweeping down like a squadron of fighter planes.

"Watch out!" warned Bertie.

"HEEEEEELP!" squawked Mr Monk, taking to his heels. The swarm of bees

Dirty Bertie

gave chase, zooming
after him. Bertie had
never seen anyone
move so fast. Mr Monk
hurdled over a flower
bed and dived head
first into a gorse bush.

Dirty Bertie

BUZZ! BUZZ! BUZZZZZZ!

The bees swept on past like a tornado and vanished into the sky.

Bertie heard muffled curses coming from the prickly bush where Mr Monk's bottom was sticking out.

"Quick, let's get out of here!" he said, grabbing the jar of honey.

They fled up the garden and out through the side gate. They didn't stop running until they reached Bertie's house. Bertie paused to get his breath and check that Mr Monk wasn't following them.

"Mr Monk will do his nut," said Darren. "You let all his bees escape!"

"It wasn't my fault," said Bertie. "If he hadn't shouted at me I wouldn't have bumped into the beehive. Anyway, I've

Dirty Bertie

changed my mind about keeping bees."

"Too dangerous!" said Eugene.

"Yes, and too much trouble," agreed
Bertie. He dipped his finger in the jar.
"From now on I think I'll just eat honey
rather than make it."

After all it was best to stick to what
you were good at.

GRANNY WARS!

CHAPTER 1

Bertie liked Wednesdays. His gran often dropped in for tea and brought a cake.

"Thanks, Gran," he said, taking another slice before Suzy had finished her first.

Mum was reading through the post from that morning.

"Oh, a postcard from Great Aunt Morag," she said, frowning.

Dirty Bertie

Bertie almost choked on his cake.

"Not Great Aunt Morag!" he said.

"What does the miserable old bat want this time?" asked Gran.

Mum read out the postcard.

POST CARD

I'm writing with splendid news:
I'm coming to stay for the
weekend, arriving on Saturday.
    Yours, Morag
      PS I missed Bertie's birthday
so I'll bring his present

Mr and Mrs Burns
Binfield Road
Pudsley
PU4 8AP

"She's coming to stay?" moaned Bertie. "*AGAIN?*"

"To be fair we haven't seen her since last Christmas," said Mum.

Dirty Bertie

Bertie wasn't likely to forget. Great
Aunt Morag had done her best to
ruin Christmas. She didn't like children
getting up early or watching TV or
playing with their presents.

"Can't you tell her we're busy?"
pleaded Suzy.

"She *is* your great aunt and she only
visits us once a year," said Mum.

"Once is enough!" muttered Bertie.

"But Saturday's the fun run," said Suzy.
"We're doing it together, Mum."

"Heavens, I forgot about that," said
Mum. "And Dad's helping out as a
marshall. What are we going to do with
Great Aunt Morag?"

Bertie burped loudly.

"Bertie's not doing anything," said
Suzy slyly.

"What?" said Bertie. "I'm not looking after her!"

"You just need to keep her company for a few hours," said Mum.

"A few *hours*?" moaned Bertie – that would seem like a lifetime! Great Aunt Morag would probably nag him to death! He should have entered the Fun Run so he had an excuse.

"I thought Bertie and I were coming to watch," said Gran.

"Well I suppose you could bring Morag along with you," suggested Mum at a loss.

"You must be joking!' said Gran. "Can you imagine Morag at a Fun Run?"

No one could. Great Aunt Morag wouldn't like the crowds or the run ... or the fun, for that matter.

"Well, we'll have to think of something," Mum sighed. "We're all going to be busy except you two. Perhaps you could play a board game together?"

"No way! It's not fair!" wailed Bertie. He didn't see why he should have his

Dirty Bertie

Saturday ruined by Great Aunt Morag. After all *he* hadn't invited her. Why did miserable relatives insist on coming to visit anyway? Why couldn't they just stay home and be miserable? There was only one crumb of comfort – his great aunt would be bringing his birthday present. He hoped it was something he actually wanted – a remote control tank, for instance.

CHAPTER 2

Early on Saturday morning the doorbell rang. Great Aunt Morag had arrived. She was wearing the same ancient flowery hat as last time and a permanent scowl.

"Great Aunt Morag!" said Mum, kissing her cheek. "Come in! How are you?"

"Exhausted. The train was late,"

grumbled Great Aunt Morag. "And the taxi from the station cost a fortune."

"Never mind, you're here now," said Dad. "Bertie, bring Great Aunt Morag's suitcase."

Bertie dragged in the suitcase, which weighed a ton. He wondered if his birthday present was inside. A remote control tank was bound to be quite heavy!

They sat in the lounge while Great Aunt Morag sipped her tea and complained about the weather.

"Well, luckily the sun's shining today because Suzy and I are doing the Fun Run this morning," said Mum.

Great Aunt Morag sniffed. "Really? I hope you're not expecting me to come and watch."

"No, of course not," said Dad. "We thought you could do something with Bertie and Gran."

"Dotty, you mean?" said Great Aunt Morag. "I might have known she'd be coming over." She scowled at Bertie. "Sit up straight and don't slouch, child! I see they're still spoiling you with drinks and biscuits."

Bertie gaped. Everyone was eating biscuits, why pick on him? Thankfully he was saved by the doorbell – Gran had arrived.

"Ah, Morag, here you are," she said, coming in. "You're looking well, a bit older and more wrinkly of course."

"Hello, Dotty," said Morag, eyeing Gran coldly. "You've put on a bit of weight, I see."

Gran and Morag had only met once
but they'd taken an instant dislike to
each other.

"So what shall we do this morning?"
asked Gran.

"What about the snowdome?"
suggested Bertie hopefully. "We could

go snowboarding!"

Great Aunt Morag gave him a withering look.

"I'm not sure Great Aunt Morag would enjoy snowboarding," said Dad quickly. "We've got plenty of board games in the cupboard."

Bertie couldn't think of anything worse – he bet his great aunt cheated at Monopoly. At least if they were outside he could run off and get away from her.

"What about Frogwood Park?" he said. "They've got a new adventure playground!"

"That's a good idea," said Gran. "There's a café and a boating lake, and they have lovely gardens too."

Great Aunt Morag almost looked interested.

Dirty Bertie

"Well as long as it's free," she said.
"And not full of noisy children."

Bertie thought there wasn't much
point to a park where children couldn't
be noisy.

Great Aunt Morag went upstairs to
get ready.

"I'm not sure I can take a whole day of
her," sighed Bertie.

"Nor me," said Gran.
"Never mind, Bertie, we'll
soon wear her out. If she
falls asleep, she might
even stop grumbling."

CHAPTER 3

As soon as they arrived at Frogwood
Park, Bertie made a beeline for the
playground. It was bigger and better than
the one at his local park. Besides the
usual swings and slides, there was a giant
spider's web climbing frame. Bertie ran
over and jumped on the swings while his
great aunt sat down on a bench.

"You sit there and rest your poor old feet, Morag," said Gran. "I'll keep an eye on Bertie."

"I'm not in the grave yet, Dotty," said Morag. "I used to love going on the swings."

"Well of course, when you were a lot younger," laughed Gran.

"I'll have you know I'm pretty active for my age," said Morag. "I go to a local keep fit class. It's called 'Move It or Lose It'."

"Sounds thrilling," said Gran. She pointed at Bertie. "But I doubt if you can still swing like that."

That did it. If there was one thing Great Aunt Morag hated, it was anyone telling her what she couldn't do. She marched over to the swings and settled

into one beside Bertie. Gran took the
remaining swing.

"What are you doing?" asked Bertie.

"What does it look like?" replied
Gran, pushing off.

"Come on! Is that the best you can
do?" cried Great Aunt Morag.

Dirty Bertie

Bertie stared in horror as the two grannies kicked up their legs, each determined to prove they could swing the highest. If this was Gran's idea of wearing his great aunt out Bertie wanted nothing to do with it. He moved to the slide pretending that he wasn't with them.

After that the morning only got worse. Whatever Gran did, Great Aunt Morag was determined to do it better. They both came off the roundabout so dizzy that they had to sit down for ten minutes. Then they noticed Bertie climbing the giant spider's web.

"You wouldn't dare," said Gran.

"Wouldn't I?" replied Great Aunt Morag. "Try and stop me."

Bertie groaned as they hitched up their dresses and began to climb.

By the time they got halfway they were both red-faced and panting for breath. Gran had a hole in her tights while Morag's hair had escaped from her hat. A small crowd gathered to watch as Bertie helped them back down.

"*Please* can we go to the café now?" he begged.

"Good idea," wheezed Gran. "I think Morag needs a rest."

They found a table in the café and looked at the menu.

"Just a small pot of tea for me," said Great Aunt Morag.

"Can we have chocolate cake?" asked Bertie.

"Of course," said Gran.

"Cake is for spoilt children," grumbled Great Aunt Morag.

Dirty Bertie

"Nonsense! He's a growing boy," argued Gran.

In the end Great Aunt Morag had her tea while Gran and Bertie shared a piece of chocolate fudge cake. As he tucked into the cake Bertie eyed his great aunt's handbag.

"Is my present in there?" he asked.

"That's for me to know," snapped Great Aunt Morag. "Patience is a virtue."

Bertie had no idea what a virtue was but he wished she'd just give him his present. How long did he have to wait? He looked out of the window at the boating lake.

"Can we take a rowing boat out?" he asked.

CHAPTER 4

SPLISH, SPLASH, SPLOSH!

Bertie sat in the back of the boat beside his great aunt, while Gran did all the rowing. For about half an hour they'd been going round in circles.

Great Aunt Morag seemed quite happy to sit back and give the orders.

"We're going left again," she tutted,

clutching her handbag. "I thought you said you could row, Dotty."

"It's hard work!" panted Gran. "You have a go if you're so clever."

"Why don't I take a turn?" offered Bertie.

"You're not old enough," said Great Aunt Morag.

"I am! I've done it before!" argued Bertie.

Actually he'd paddled on a lilo at the seaside, but it was almost the same thing. In any case, rowing looked dead easy. All you did was splosh the oars into the water, lean back and puff out your cheeks.

Gran slumped back, exhausted.

"I need a break," she groaned. "You change places with me, Bertie."

Dirty Bertie

This wasn't as easy as it sounded. Bertie jumped up quickly which made the boat rock from side to side.

"Watch out, you'll sink us!" squawked Great Aunt Morag.

Bertie edged forwards and performed an awkward dance with Gran as they attempted to swap places. The boat dipped to one side as they stumbled into each other. Great Aunt Morag hung on for dear life.

"SIT DOWN, FOR HEAVEN'S
SAKE!" she screeched.

Gran fell into the seat beside Morag
while Bertie sat down heavily at the
front. Now for the oars, he thought. He
grabbed one and swung it into place,
narrowly missing Great Aunt Morag's
head. As she clung to the side of the
boat her handbag slipped from her grasp.

SPLOSH!

"Now look what you've done! My
purse is in there!" she cried.

*Never mind the
purse, what about
my birthday present?*
thought Bertie.
He'd waited all
morning and
now it was about

to sink before his eyes! He leaned out, trying to reach it.

"Out of the way, I'll handle this," snapped Great Aunt Morag, grabbing one of the oars. She stood up shakily and tried to fish the handbag out of the water. But it bobbed away like a cork.

"Careful, you're tipping us over!" warned Gran.

"Oh stop fussing!" snapped Great Aunt Morag, leaning over. "If I can just get a bit— ARRRRGH!"

Great Aunt Morag gave a strangled cry as she lost her balance, flapped her arms and toppled into the lake head first.

KERSPLASH!

Luckily it turned out that the water was only waist deep. She sat up, spluttering and gasping with her hair in her eyes and her glasses misted up.

Bertie reached out and grabbed her handbag as it floated by.

"LOOK WHAT YOU'VE DONE!" choked Great Aunt Morag as a pair of curious ducks swam round her.

"*Me?*" said Bertie. "I didn't do anything. You're the one who fell in!"

Dirty Bertie

At least he'd managed to rescue her handbag, you'd think she'd be grateful.

Some time later they arrived home. Suzy, Mum and Dad were back from the Fun Run and having a cup of tea in the kitchen.

"Hello," said Mum. "How was the… Oh good heavens!"

She caught sight of Great Aunt Morag's furious face and dripping wet clothes.

"What happened?" asked Dad.

"Don't ask," said Gran.

Great Aunt Morag threw down her handbag and wrung water from her soggy hat.

"I am going upstairs to change," she announced. "While I am gone you can order me a taxi to the station!"

She stomped upstairs leaving behind a puddle on the kitchen floor.

Before long she was back again, with her suitcase packed.

"I'm so sorry, Morag. Are you sure you have to go so soon?" asked Mum.

"I wouldn't stay here another minute," seethed Great Aunt Morag. "I doubt if my nerves would stand it."

"You're not the only one," said Gran.

Dirty Bertie

"Bye bye then."

Bertie and his family followed Great Aunt Morag out to the road where the taxi was waiting. Bertie carried her handbag – this was his last chance.

"Haven't you forgotten something?" he asked. "What about my birthday present?"

Great Aunt Morag glared at him. "I'm sure you don't deserve anything at all," she said. "But since I've carried it all this way, I suppose you may as well have it."

She reached into her handbag and handed him a soggy package. Bertie excitedly tore off the paper.

"Oh," he said. "What is it?"

"A bowl of course," replied Great Aunt Morag. "I made it myself at pottery class. What do you say, ungrateful child?"

"Um, thanks," sighed Bertie. He'd put up with Great Aunt Morag all day, but instead of a remote control tank his reward was a lumpy pottery bowl.

"Enjoy it, because it's the last present you'll ever get from me," said Great Aunt Morag.

They watched in silence as the taxi drove off down the road.

"What exactly did you do to her, Bertie?" asked Dad.

"Nothing! Why's everyone blaming me?" protested Bertie. "It was Gran who kept arguing with her all morning. Then she fell in the lake and moaned about it all the way home. Most people

Dirty Bertie

would have found it funny."

"I know I did," grinned Gran. "It was the highlight of the day! So what are you going to do with your present, Bertie?"

Bertie thought for a moment. "You know what – Whiffer needs a new bowl."

Gran laughed. "A dog bowl – perfect! I'm sure Morag would be thrilled."

BARKING!

Best
Local
Newspaper
Column

CHAPTER 1

Bertie and his family were eating supper.

"Great news!" said Mum excitedly. "I've won an award."

A blob of mashed potato fell off Bertie's fork.

"What sort of award?" he asked.

"Best Local Newspaper Column of the Year," replied Mum.

Bertie was astonished. His mum hadn't been working for the local paper very long. He'd been going to school for years and he'd never won a single thing!

"That's amazing, Mum," said Suzy.

"Isn't it great?" said Dad proudly.

"What's the prize?" asked Bertie. He hoped it was a thousand pounds, then he could buy a hamster.

"Just a trophy with my name on," said Mum. "But the best part is the awards dinner is at a four-star hotel. Dad and I will be staying the night."

"But what about *us*?" moaned Bertie.

"You?" said Mum.

"Yes, aren't we invited?" asked Suzy.

"I'm sure you'd be bored at an awards dinner," said Dad quickly. "It'll be lots of long speeches with people thanking everyone they know."

"I don't mind, especially if we can stay in a four-star hotel!" said Bertie.

He'd stayed in a caravan once but he doubted if it had four stars. At the hotel they'd probably have their own private swimming pool with a butler to bring them breakfast!

Dirty Bertie

"*Pleeeease*," begged Suzy. "We want to cheer you on."

"Yes, it won't be the same without us," argued Bertie.

Mum looked at Dad and sighed.

"Well it's not often I win an award," she said. "I suppose I *could* ask for a couple of extra tickets."

"Yahoo!" cried Bertie, sending peas bouncing across the table. This was amazing – they were actually going to stay in a FOUR-STAR HOTEL. He hoped the awards dinner would be burger and chips!

Whiffer padded over and rested his head in Bertie's lap.

Dirty Bertie

"Oh, what about Whiffer? Can he come too?" asked Bertie.

"Definitely not!" said Mum.

"Four-star hotels don't allow dogs," said Dad.

"Why not? I could look after him!" argued Bertie.

"It's out of the question," said Mum. "Whiffer's not coming and that's final."

Bertie sighed. Whiffer was part of the family so it didn't seem fair to leave him behind. If *Bertie* ran a hotel all dogs would be welcome and any other pets for that matter. Maybe not crocodiles though, they might cause a problem in the swimming pool.

CHAPTER 2

On Saturday they packed their bags
ready to set off. Whiffer drooped
around the house, watching them
miserably. He always seemed to know
when they were going away. In the
kitchen Mum almost tripped over him.

"Is Gran okay to feed Whiffer?" she
asked Dad. "You did phone her?"

Dirty Bertie

"Me? I thought *you* were doing it," said Dad.

"We talked about this," groaned Mum. "Do I have to do *everything*?"

Bertie left his parents to argue and took Whiffer into the hall.

"I'm sorry you can't come," he said. "*I'd* let you but the mean hotel has stupid rules about dogs."

Whiffer hung his head. Bertie imagined him moping around the house all weekend with no one to play with. It just wasn't fair. The front door was open and the car sat waiting on the drive. Bertie suddenly had a brainwave. Posh hotels didn't allow dogs but what if they didn't know anything about it?

"Wait there, I'll be back in a minute," he told Whiffer.

Dirty Bertie

Finally they were ready to leave. Mum opened the car door and found Bertie sitting on the back seat. He had his favourite duvet spread across his legs.

"What's that for?" asked Mum. "They'll have duvets at the hotel."

"I know but I can't get to sleep without it," replied Bertie.

Suzy rolled her eyes and climbed in beside him.

Dad started the engine. "Gran promised she'd pop in later to feed Whiffer," he said. "Where is he by the way?"

"Oh, he's, um … on my bed," replied Bertie quickly. "I think he's sulking."

He glanced down at the duvet covering his legs. A head-shaped lump popped up and Bertie carefully pushed it down. Luckily nobody was looking.

They set off and were soon out of town. As they joined the motorway, Mum wrinkled her nose. "What's that funny smell?" she sniffed. "It's sort of doggy."

"I can't smell anything," said Bertie innocently.

Dirty Bertie

"It's probably Bertie's stinky duvet," said Suzy. "Whiffer's always sleeping on it."

Bertie kept his mouth shut. If they could just make it to the hotel, then his plan had a chance of success. Glancing down, he noticed the duvet had slipped and two large, brown eyes were peering up at him. He quickly covered Whiffer's head but not fast enough.

"EEEK!" screamed Suzy.

Dirty Bertie

Mum turned round.

"What's the matter?" she asked.

"Nothing!" said Bertie. He looked at Suzy, begging her not to give the game away.

"It's okay," she said. "Bertie elbowed me, that's all."

Mum sighed heavily. "*Please* try not to annoy each other, it's not far now."

Bertie shot his sister a grateful look. It wasn't like Suzy not to tell tales. Maybe she knew that turning back now would cause an almighty row and ruin Mum's special day.

CHAPTER 3

At last they pulled into the sweeping driveway of Hotel Majestic. Bertie was impressed with the grand entrance lined with flags. It looked like the sort of place the Queen went on holiday.

Dad parked in the car park and everyone except Bertie got out. Now what? He hadn't planned any further than getting to the hotel. The moment anyone heard a dog barking they'd be rumbled.

Dad looked in at him.

"Are you coming or not?" he said.

"Me? Oh yes. I'll just fold my duvet and I'll catch you up," said Bertie.

"You go in," sighed Suzy. "I'll wait for slowcoach."

Their parents headed for the hotel entrance, wheeling their suitcases behind them.

"You're out of your mind," said Suzy.

"He *wanted* to come," replied Bertie. "You won't tell, will you?"

"No, but you owe me," said Suzy. "I get choice of beds and control of the TV."

Bertie nodded. He was hardly in a position to bargain. Whiffer pulled on his lead, wanting to run off and play.

"So, genius, how do you plan to sneak him inside?" asked Suzy.

It was a good question. The minute they stepped through the door they'd probably set off a million alarm bells.

"I'll think of something," said Bertie. "Tell Mum and Dad I've gone to the loo."

In the end Bertie decided he'd just have to carry Whiffer wrapped in the duvet. It was harder than it sounded. Whiffer weighed a ton and kept wriggling about, trying to escape. People turned to stare as Bertie pushed

Dirty Bertie

in through the revolving doors. He staggered past reception, half hidden by the enormous duvet.

"May I help you with that, sir?"

Bertie froze. A hotel porter was smiling at him, blocking his path.

"It's okay," panted Bertie. "It's just my duvet."

"I can see that, but let me help you, sir," insisted the man.

Bertie heard a PING. The lift doors were opening.

"I've got it, thanks," Bertie mumbled, dodging past. He jumped in and the doors slid shut behind him. Whiffer scrambled free and barked excitedly.

"You're not really helping," said Bertie.

They went up and down in the lift three or four times trying to find Suzy. At last Bertie spotted her hanging around on the fifth floor landing.

"Where have you *been*?" she hissed. "Mum and Dad are looking for you."

"I didn't know which floor we were on," explained Bertie.

They hurried down the corridor with Whiffer stopping to explore all the new smells.

Suzy pointed. "We're in here, Room 501," she said. "But he can't sleep with us."

"I s'pose not," sighed Bertie. "So what can we do?"

"Don't ask me! It was your stupid idea to bring him," said Suzy.

They were in luck. Along the corridor,

the door to Room 506 had been left open. Bertie peered inside.

"It's empty," he said. "We can leave him in here."

"What if someone comes?" asked Suzy.

"Then we'll just have to move him," said Bertie.

He dragged Whiffer inside and left him a supply of dog biscuits.

"I'll be back soon," Bertie explained. "Stay here and don't make a noise."

He left the door slightly ajar so he could get back in.

"You realize they'll throw us out if they find him," warned Suzy. "Mum will miss getting her award."

Bertie hadn't thought of that. He'd just have to make sure Whiffer stayed a secret.

CHAPTER 4

Downstairs they found Mum and Dad in reception, looking agitated.

"Where on earth have you been, Bertie?" asked Dad.

"I got lost trying to find the room!" said Bertie, which was partly true.

"Well for heaven's sake don't wander off again," said Mum. "Dinner's at six and I need to practise my speech."

They sat down in the lounge and listened as she ran through it.

"It's perfect," said Dad. "You'll be fine."

"They'll all love it," said Suzy.

"Yes," said Bertie. "Although it'd be better with more jokes."

"There *were* jokes," said Mum.

"Yes, but I mean funny ones," said Bertie. "Like, what's red and invisible?"

They never heard the answer because a man in a shiny blue suit interrupted. Mum introduced him as her boss at the newspaper, Mr Williams.

"The funniest thing just happened," he said. "I found a dog in my room!"

"A *dog?*" said Mum.

"Yes, just lying on the bed as if the room was *his!*" chuckled Mr Williams.

Dirty Bertie

"I've no idea how he got there!"

Bertie thought he had a pretty good idea.

"How extraordinary!" said Dad. "What sort of dog?"

"Black and white, a bit smelly," said Mr Williams. "Anyway, he ran off when he saw me. I've reported it to the hotel."

Dirty Bertie

Mum frowned. "We've got a dog like that but we left him at home," she said.

"Yes, good job he's not here!" said Bertie. "Actually, I just need the loo again."

"You just went!" groaned Mum. "Hurry up, we'll need to get changed before dinner."

Bertie charged off. This was a disaster! How was he to know Mum's boss was staying in Room 506? Whiffer could be anywhere by now – and Mr Williams had reported a dog in the hotel. Bertie had to find him before anyone else did. Where to start though? There were seven floors and a million rooms!

Bertie searched every meeting room and landing but with no success. At six he hurried to join his family for dinner.

"There you are!" cried Dad.

Dirty Bertie

"And you haven't even changed!" groaned Mum, pointing to his jeans.

"I ... er ... I got locked in the toilets," said Bertie.

Mum rolled her eyes. "Just stay in your seat and don't move," she said.

"Well?" Suzy whispered as they sat down. Bertie shook his head and scanned the room. Knowing Whiffer he'd be sniffing around for food by now.

The dimly lit room was set up with a dozen round tables all facing the head table. Behind it was a long velvet curtain. Bertie slurped the soup in his bowl. Yuck! *It wasn't even hot!* The main course was a choice of stinky fish or chicken served in a sloppy sauce – not a burger in sight. *Pretty rubbish for a four-star hotel,* thought Bertie.

Dirty Bertie

After dessert, a tall woman in a black dress got up to announce the awards. People were called up to the front and made long, boring speeches without any jokes. Suddenly Bertie saw a flash of white fur passing the open doorway. Whiffer! In his excitement Bertie knocked over a glass of red wine. OOOPS! He grabbed the nearest napkin and tried to mop it up. Just then the woman read out his mum's name.

"Goodness!" Mum gulped. "Where's my speech?"

Her eyes fell on the soggy napkin and she gasped. Bertie stared. It wasn't a napkin at all, it was Mum's notes!

"My speech!" shrieked Mum. "How could you do this?"

"Sorry, it was an accident," said Bertie.

Mum groaned. "Why do I never learn? I knew something like this would happen if we brought you!" She hurried up to the front, clutching her soggy notes.

"Thank you so much," said Mum breathlessly. "If I can er … read my writing I do have a few people to thank. First of all…"

Bertie wasn't listening. He was staring at the velvet curtain behind her, which kept moving.

Whiffer! thought Bertie. He knew he wouldn't be able to resist the smell of food for long. While everyone was listening to Mum, Bertie slipped out of the door behind him and crept back in through a door near the front. He wasn't far from the curtain now. If he crawled on all fours maybe he could grab Whiffer and escape unseen. He got down on his hands and knees.

"Finally," said Mum, "I'd like to thank my husband and two lovely children—"

Dirty Bertie

THUMP!

WOOF! WOOF! WOOF!

Her speech was drowned out by some sort of scuffle behind the curtain. The tall woman pulled it back. Bertie lay on the floor, wrestling with Whiffer who had a chicken drumstick in his mouth.

"BERTIE!" groaned Mum.

"Oh, hi," said Bertie. "Look who I found."

He struggled to his feet, leaving
Whiffer to slobber over his drumstick.

The room had fallen deathly silent.
Everyone stared open-mouthed.
Bertie felt that somebody ought to
say something. He crossed to the
microphone.

"So anyway," he said.
"What's red and invisible?
No tomatoes!"